henry

ELISHA COOPER

henry

CHRONICLE BOOKS

SAN FRANCISCO

Library of Congress Cataloging-in-Publication Data available.

ISBN 0-8118-2402-0

Printed in Hong Kong.

Designed by ANNE GALPERIN

Distributed in Canada by Raincoast Books
8680 Cambie Street
Vancouver, British Columbia V6P 6M9

10 9 8 7 6 5 4 3 2 1

Chronicle Books
85 Second Street
San Francisco, California 94105

www.chroniclebooks.com

i GREW UP on a farm. It sat on the side of a hill and had an apple orchard, a pond, and long fields that ran into forests. It also had cows and cats, bees and goats, a dog, a

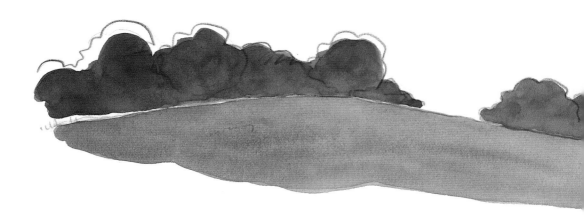

barn, and the house where my family lived. On a spring morning when I was ten, our dog had puppies. One I liked more than the others and his name was Henry.

hENRY SPENT HIS first weeks in a ball of siblings, nursed from his mother, and grew. Henry's paws got so big he didn't know where to put them; they just flopped out behind. Some parts of Henry grew at different speeds: one day his paws were larger than the rest of him, one day it was his skin, another day it was his stomach.

hENRY HAD AN ear that turned inside out and a slightly bent tail. He never seemed completely dressed. With dark thoughtful eyes and tawny yellow fur, he looked like a small, nice lion. We gave his brothers and sisters away when they were two months old, but Henry stayed. Henry belonged to me, though after a while I belonged to him.

WHEN HENRY LEARNED to run he chased his mother in circles. Then she chased him and he ran, tail between his legs. They rolled down the hill entwined as one body until they hit the stone wall at the bottom. They growled and snapped their teeth at each other, but if distracted they would stop, lean against each other, and look up. Often, Henry lay right on top of her.

SOMETIMES HENRY WANDERED off on his own and sat at the top of the hill. From there he could look over the whole farm. He seemed to like this place. He would blink his eyes, let the wind run through his hair, and listen to the fields and the stories they were telling him. Perhaps he thought about lunch.

WHEN IT WAS time for me to feed him, Henry leapt up and down and fell over. He shook his whole rear end while he ate. Then he drank from the bowl in the kitchen, stood in it with his two front paws, splashed water on the floor, and lay in it for a post-lunch bath.

H ENRY STILL SPENT most of his time growing and sleeping, stretching into different positions while he dreamt. If he had nightmares I woke him. When he got up he looked perplexed for a moment, both ears flopped inside out. He learned to go out onto the field in the middle of the night, sniff around, dump or pee. He learned his name, learned to sit, learned to come when called.

i N THE FALL, Henry unearthed molehills and brought home antlers that deer had shed. He teethed on rocks, bones, work boots, and sticks that waited for him where he had left them the day before. His favorite was his mother's ears. One morning Henry chewed on grass and spent the afternoon throwing up.

tHE GOATS AND I and Henry and Henry's mother took
walks around the farm, each day a bit farther. Once we
made it all the way down to the pond, and Henry splashed

at the edge. The next day he waded out into the water
and went in over his head. He came up swimming though,
surprised at himself. Everything was new for Henry.

WHEN HENRY WAS a year old he got his first collar. It was small and simple and had a metal tag that said "Henry." It also said where he lived. Henry didn't like the collar at first, trying hard to bend his neck and chew it, but after a while it made him proud and he shook it when he walked.

tHE SNOW WAS fascinating in Henry's first winter. He wallowed in it, chased snowballs I threw, and slid after his mother. When he sneezed he sent plumes of frost into the cold air.

OUR NEIGHBORS' CHICKENS interested Henry. He stared at the roosters as they strutted around the barnyard. Once he caught one and brought it home in his mouth. Henry was gentle and the bird was unhurt, though startled, and it flew down the hill fast when I told Henry, "Let go."

SEX BEGAN TO interest Henry too. In May he jumped his mother, who barked, and my leg when I wasn't watching, and a cat, who scratched him, and the goats, who butted him. One weekend he went away. We thought he was lost, but Henry came back two days later with an air about him like he'd accomplished something.

hENRY WAS ALMOST full size. If no one was in the kitchen Henry stretched his body up on the table and looked for leftovers. If no one was home Henry went to the barn, tipped over the garbage cans, and ate everything he could find.

ONE EVENING HENRY and his mother howled and scratched at the door, begging to be let out. Something was outside. When they returned an hour later they looked sheepish and smelled of skunk. They spent the next two hours in the bathtub with three cans of tomato juice, but the smell lingered for days.

h ENRY WENT INTO the fields one day and chased the cows. The cows stampeded, lowing and looking worried, their udders bouncing heavily back and forth beneath them. When Henry came back he looked happy, but guilty too. And after I scolded him he spent the rest of the day trying to gain back my approval.

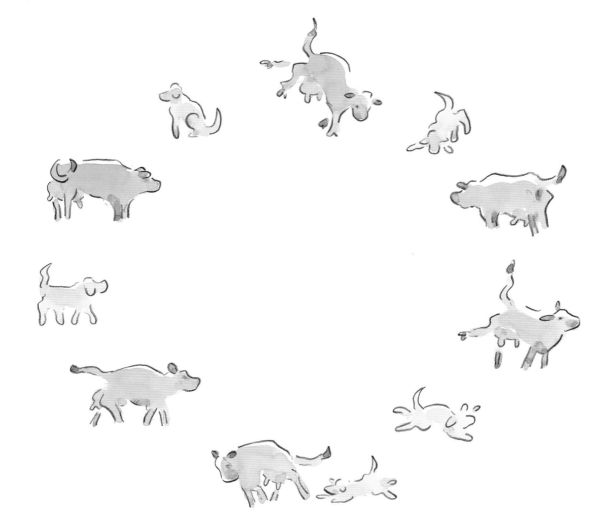

h ENRY'S MOTHER WAS better than Henry at chasing balls. When I threw for her at the pond, Henry waited at the bank, and when she came back he pounced and stole the ball away from her. Most of the time Henry swam in circles, just enjoying the motion, or rummaged in the marshy edges where the bullfrogs hid.

---

iN NOVEMBER I went running with Henry, who dashed into the underbrush if he sensed deer, rushed to catch up with me, then raced ahead, his tongue flapping alongside him. He stopped to watch geese flying over the farm, their wings beating the air and their honks filling it.

iN HENRY'S SECOND winter I got a sled and flew up and down the hill, carving turns in the snow. Henry and his mother bounded behind, and we sledded into the evening,

coming back to eat and rest by the stove in the kitchen. Sometimes we sledded in the moonlight.

iN THE SPRING, Henry helped my mother pull the hose out to the garden. While she planted seeds he rooted between the rows with his nose. Then he napped in the shade of the green beans and tomatoes, and listened to crickets.

WHEN HENRY WANTED his belly scratched, he rolled over and revved his back paw at me. Henry sometimes itched himself for fun, panting when he was done and barking at nothing in particular. Once he had fleas and had to go to the vet for a spraying.

itching

licking
himself

h ENRY WASN'T A good fighter. He came home one night cut and bleeding, beaten up by a raccoon, and had to go to the vet. A neighbor's dog also beat up Henry, turning his bent ear into a tattered curtain. The goats had to rush in and butt the dog away.

IN THE DOG days of summer the pond was too hot for swimming. So Henry lay flat in the nearby bog, cooling his belly in the mud. When he came out he was a two-toned dog. If it was too hot to go to the bog, Henry slunk out to the barn, and stretched on the cold concrete in the shade of the manure pile.

OUR FAMILY WENT on a trip to the city and brought Henry and his mother along. He didn't like the traffic, didn't like being on a leash, was curious about one pack of dogs, and was happy to get back to the farm.

dURING JULY, THE hay fields were mown. It took all
day. A tractor cut the waving hay flat, then spun it
into rows that Henry hurdled, then into bales. I stacked the

bales into forts, which then were loaded onto a creaky wooden wagon and taken to the barn and stored. Henry walked behind the wagon, his nose in the air.

i CUT APPLE branches in the fall and dragged them to the barn for the goats to eat. Henry pulled a branch too, tugging one twice his size. When he was done he took a nap underneath the apple trees, not bothered by nesting swallows who dove at him.

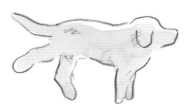

eVEN IF I didn't join him, Henry walked around the farm anyway and checked to make sure everything was all right. He lifted his leg to mark his territory and scruffed up the ground behind him.

On December mornings, before the sun came up, Henry walked with me over icy ground out to the barn to milk the goats. While I fed the goats — their milk hissing into metal buckets — Henry went into the stall and ate their droppings.

aFTER EATING ORNAMENTS off the tree during a holiday blizzard and being sent outside, Henry waded through drifts to the top of the hill. A cat came too and passed back and forth under Henry's nose with her tail until he relented and licked her face.

WHEN HENRY STOPPED thinking he chased bees. In April, blossoms bloomed and bees cruised from bud to bud, and Henry trotted up to the apple orchard. He sat very still, and when a bee flew by his head, he snapped his jaws — with a loud clomping sound — and the bee was gone.

h ENRY SHED IN the spring. His fur came out in clumps and had a way of following me to school. Most of it, though, floated into the fields, where birds used it for nests. I once found a swallow's nest in the barn made of twigs, mud, and Henry's hair.

On sunday mornings, the goats and Henry and Henry's mother and I walked to the mailbox and got the paper. We sat at the top of the hill and read and the goats grazed. After a while, Henry's mother grew impatient and stared at her ball until I threw it. Then Henry loped after her.

OUR FAMILY WENT on a longer trip, and Henry had to stay behind to watch the farm. And though the neighbors who came to feed him were nice enough, they said that Henry seemed distracted and would walk up to the mailbox alone, and wait, and listen for the sounds of a returning car.

i N OCTOBER, OUR family made cider, climbing ladders
and dropping apples into bushel baskets that we
dragged down the hill to the barn to be pressed. I threw

rotten apples for Henry. He didn't have to return them and
chewed them by himself.

OUR HOUSE HAD no locks, and whenever someone came over Henry went outside to see who it was. But he wasn't much of a watchdog, and more often than not would invite strangers inside, gently holding their hands in his mouth, and point out to them his bowl, his bed, where the food was kept.

drool —

WHEN OUR FAMILY ate dinner, Henry stared at the table, concentrating on each dish as it was passed, trying to look neglected. A strand of saliva stretched from his mouth to the floor. Henry helped clean the dishes, locking one paw inside the bowl, the other outside to steady it. His ears, even the one that flopped inside out, fell over the edge of the bowl. Henry did such a good job of licking the dishes that once I put them back just like that, and never told anyone, though I only did this once.

iF I HAD a bad day at school, or if things went wrong, I knew I could go to the top of the hill and find Henry. I could knead Henry's coat, and Henry would lick my face, and I would feel better. Henry leaned on me.

tHE YEARS STRETCHED on and I went away to college, but when I came home for vacation Henry was so excited he turned himself inside out. And though Henry was older now, his joints more tired, he raced around in circles a few times like he had when he was a puppy. We went for walks together, thoughtful walks, with fewer rushes into the bushes for deer.

Without me, Henry spent his days walking around the farm, saying hello to the goats, and getting climbed on by the neighbors' children. Only when they were done did he lumber up the hill to rest, or think about lunch. Maybe he made up stories.

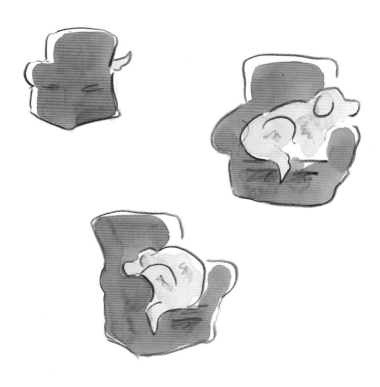

h ENRY'S COAT WAS still tawny, but some days it looked like the hay fields after a rain — lying down in spots, with different patches going different ways. More and more he liked being petted. In the evenings Henry slept in a comfortable chair or by the stove in the kitchen, dreaming.

$\mathbf{i}$ F I CALLED home I asked how Henry was. My parents would tell me, and Henry would listen, knowing he was being talked about. Then he would ask to be let outside, to bark at the moon or some far-off animal. And my parents would say, "That's Henry."

H ENRY MADE FEWER trips now to upset the trash cans. He sat under the bird feeder and waited for messy birds. One night, when my parents were out, Henry got into the food bin and ate until he almost burst. When they came home, Henry was in pain, so they called the vet. The vet came over, and after checking Henry, said that Henry's stomach was contorted and that Henry's body, well used over the years, wouldn't survive an operation. It was Henry's way of saying it was time.

So they decided to put Henry to sleep, though it wasn't an easy decision. I imagine the vet told Henry what he was doing, and Henry looked at him with his dark eyes, and the vet gently inserted the needle, and Henry went still. Then my parents called me at school to tell me that Henry was dead.

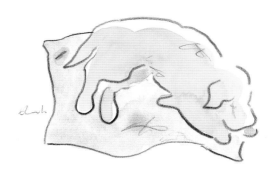

S O I CAME home to bury Henry on a beautiful spring morning. I wrapped his body in a blanket and brought him to the top of the hill. From the barn I got a shovel, and dug a deep grave under the apple trees at the spot that looked out over the farm where Henry liked to sit. Henry's mother, and the cats, and the goats stood by quietly and watched. They knew what was happening.

As swallows flew overhead, I took Henry's body, lighter now, and laid it in the bottom of the grave. And I patted Henry's head and straightened his one floppy ear, and talked softly about our walks together, the times we had sat together, looking out over the farm. Then I touched Henry one last time, tossed in some dirt, then shoveled more, until the earth was whole again. I sat for a good while on the hill and my animals gathered round.

hE is still with me.

Elise Cappella

ELISHA COOPER is the author and illustrator of *A Year in New York, Off the Road: An American Sketchbook,* and *A Day at Yale,* as well as several children's books, including *Ballpark* and *Building.* He lives in Northern California.